Dear Parent:

Congratulations! Your child is taking the first steps on an exciting journey. The destination? Independent reading!

STEP INTO READING® will help your child get there. The program offers five steps to reading success. Each step includes fun stories and colorful art. There are also Step into Reading Sticker Books, Step into Reading Math Readers, Step into Reading Write-In Readers, Step into Reading Phonics Readers, and Step into Reading Phonics First Steps! Boxed Sets—a complete literacy program with something for every child.

Learning to Read, Step by Step!

Ready to Read   **Preschool–Kindergarten**
• big type and easy words • rhyme and rhythm • picture clues
For children who know the alphabet and are eager to begin reading.

Reading with Help   **Preschool–Grade 1**
• basic vocabulary • short sentences • simple stories
For children who recognize familiar words and sound out new words with help.

Reading on Your Own   **Grades 1–3**
• engaging characters • easy-to-follow plots • popular topics
For children who are ready to read on their own.

Reading Paragraphs   **Grades 2–3**
• challenging vocabulary • short paragraphs • exciting stories
For newly independent readers who read simple sentences with confidence.

Ready for Chapters   **Grades 2–4**
• chapters • longer paragraphs • full-color art
For children who want to take the plunge into chapter books but still like colorful pictures.

STEP INTO READING® is designed to give every child a successful reading experience. The grade levels are only guides. Children can progress through the steps at their own speed, developing confidence in their reading, no matter what their grade. Remember, a lifetime love of reading starts with a single step!

Thomas the Tank Engine & Friends™

CREATED BY BRITT ALLCROFT

Based on The Railway Series by The Reverend W Awdry.
© 2008 Gullane (Thomas) LLC.

HIT entertainment

Visit us on the Web!
www.stepintoreading.com
www.thomasandfriends.com

Educators and librarians, for a variety of teaching tools, visit us at
www.randomhouse.com/teachers

Library of Congress Cataloging-in-Publication Data
The close shave / [illustrated by Richard Courtney]. — 1st ed.
    p. cm. — (Step into reading)
"Based on The Railway Series by The Reverend W Awdry."
"Thomas the Tank Engine & Friends created by Britt Allcroft."
Summary: Thomas's friend and fellow engine, Duck, has a close shave while trying to stop runaway trucks.
ISBN 978-0-375-85180-3 (trade) — ISBN 978-0-375-95180-0 (lib. bdg.)
[1. Railroad trains—Fiction. 2. Trucks—Fiction.] I. Courtney, Richard, ill. II. Awdry, W. Railway series. III. Thomas the tank engine and friends.
PZ7.C62387 2008   [E]—dc22   2007029800

Printed in the United States of America
10 9 8 7 6 5 4 3
First Edition

The Close Shave

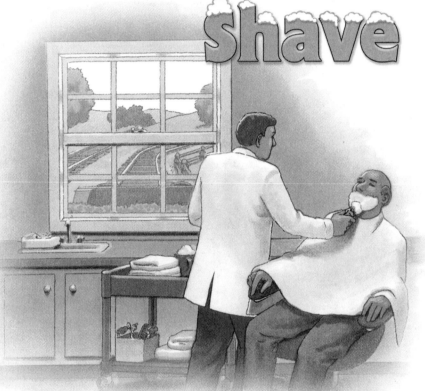

Based on *The Railway Series*
by the Reverend W Awdry

Illustrated by Richard Courtney

Random House 🏠 New York

Thomas and Duck
are friends.

They are
not friends with the
Troublesome Trucks.

They like
to chug up hills.

They like
to zip down hills.

One day,
Duck was zipping
down a hill.
Hello, Thomas!

Duck heard

a warning whistle.

"Peeeeeep! Peeeeeep!"

Trucks had run away
from Thomas.

Go, Duck!
No! Trucks!

The Trucks
bumped Duck.

14

Mad Duck!

Glad Trucks!

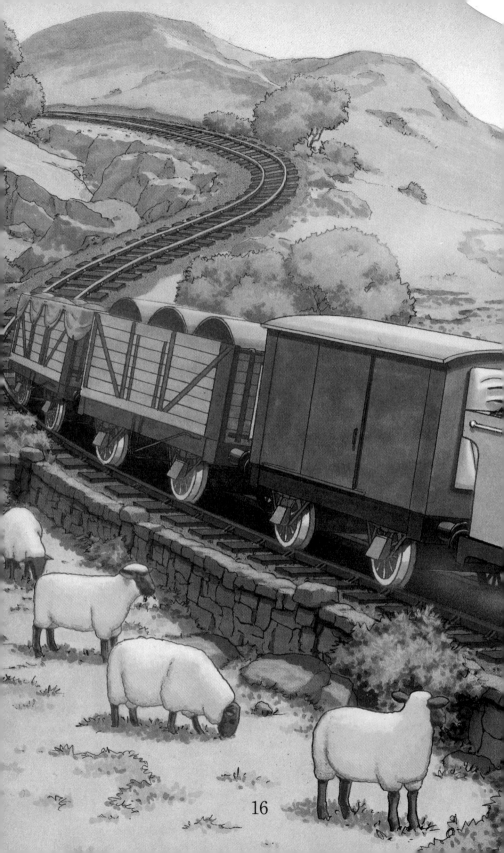

Duck and the Trucks
rushed down the hill.

Duck saw
the end of the line.
Duck had to stop!

Duck crashed
into the barber shop.

Sad Duck!
Bad Trucks!

The barber

was cross.

Soapy Duck.

Dopey Trucks!

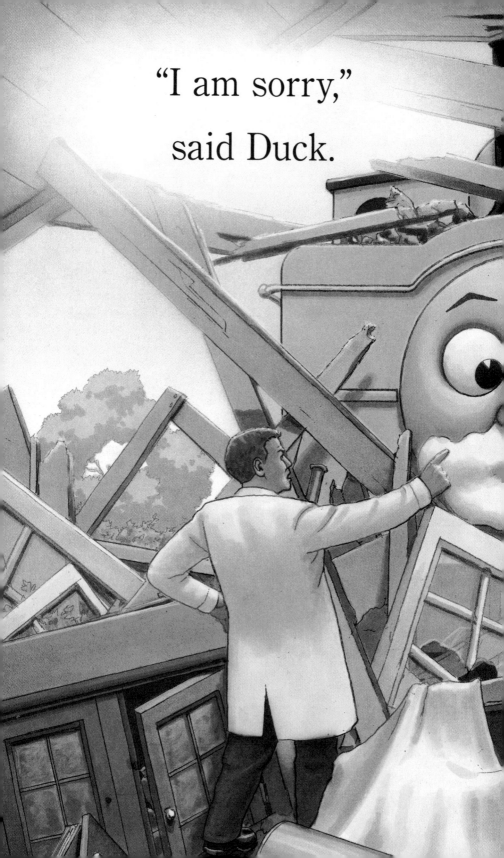

"I had to stop
the runaway Trucks."

No one was hurt.

The shop could be fixed.

Duck was a hero!

Duck got cleaned up.

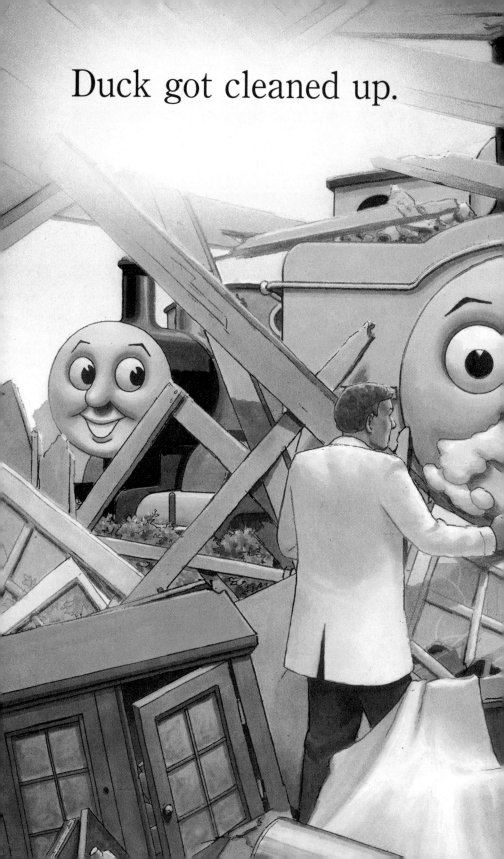

The Trucks
got picked up.

Duck had
a close shave!